TOR
WYOMING BIGHORN

TOR
WYOMING BIGHORN

by Ernestine N. Byrd

Illustrated by Donald Carrick

CHARLES SCRIBNER'S SONS / NEW YORK

To my daughter, Barbara Lee Anderson

Contents

1. The Young Must Learn

The Wind River Mountains, highest in Wyoming, their rugged peaks still tipped with snow, were outlined darkly against the first gray light of dawn. As the rays of the rising sun began to tint the sky with delicate streaks of gold, Wise One, an old ewe, leader of a small band of bighorns, stood on a crag staring fixedly across a canyon, her rough winter coat a pale shaft of grayish-white against slate-colored rocks. She was content. The spreading warmth of May had come again, bringing with it an abundance of new grass. A mountain shoulder that faced south offered grazing for the day.

Bounding from the crag, Wise One vaulted a narrow chasm and walked along the edge of a second high cliff, six ewes and a pair of two-year-old rams following. Stopping once, she looked around carefully, then leaped down the front of the cliff from tiny ledge to tiny ledge until she came to a spur of ground that led to a plateau and the rolling swell of the mountain shoulder below. Dew was still on the grass and clung in irridescent drops on clumps of white sage. The sheep licked the leaves of the sage first, then broke off the stems and chewed them, afterwards feeding on the sweet-tasting grass.

Only Tara, a young ewe, did not eat. She was heavy with her unborn lamb and felt the birth pangs beginning within her. Preferring to be alone when her time came, she returned to the plateau and chose a ledge-cove protected by rocks and brush where the cold wind blowing off the snow banks above timber line would not strike her. It was also a lookout point from which she could see the approach of any possible enemy. Here she stood quietly for several minutes, head down, legs widespread; then she lay down. A half hour later her lamb, Tor, was born. He was a long-legged, flat-sided little thing, with a pair of brown eyes, a grayish-brown coat, and a dark stripe down his back.

Tara got up and sniffed her first-born with cautious interest. At the touch and smell of his wet coat she began cleaning him from head to foot—a ewe's way of accepting her lamb. In an hour his coat was fluffed and dried with the steady motions of her tongue and he was ready to nurse. Instinct, as old as life itself, made his tottering legs carry him under her belly, where he made several weak attempts before reaching her twin-peaked udder. Tara's amber-colored eyes could see far into the distance and were her main source of protection. Now they searched the sky for the deadly shadows of Golden Eagles that could suddenly become the whirr and whistle of wings above grasping talons.

During the first week of Tor's life, Tara watched over him constantly. In between her own hasty feedings she nursed him every hour or so for a period of from twenty to thirty seconds at a time. Although each feeding was brief, he was well nourished and grew so fast that he soon had to drop to his knees in order to reach her teats. The flat-sided look became rounded, and the slender but sturdy legs carried him speedily over the rim rocks. His front feet were larger than his hind ones, for the climbing and checking of headlong dashes down hill would be done chiefly with his forelegs and feet. The bottom of each cloven hoof was concave, the edge sharp, forming a suction cup that enabled him to climb up and down the most forbidding formations of jutting ledges and sheer cliffs, as well as surfaces that were hard, soft, or slippery.

8

At first Tara kept Tor on the nursery ledge, but when he was two weeks old and strong enough to follow her, she took him out on a plateau where he joined the main flock. He eyed the two-year-old rams, Roc and Ute, with lively interest and took a few steps in their direction, but when his mother butted his rump he understood he was to leave them alone. Three lambs his own age —two females, Popo and Meta, and Arn, a male—trotted over and butted him mischievously, which was an invitation for a mock battle. With woolly head against woolly head and with pink-lobed ears laid back as if they were really angry, they pushed one another back and forth, rumps up, short tails wagging excitedly. The game of getting acquainted was so much fun that they bumped and butted and chased each other tirelessly until their mothers made them stop.

Like all baby lambs, Tor played from morning until night, but no activity was as exciting as following his mother up and down the high cliffs, landing on tiny projections, little rocky shelves, or ribbon-thin ledges—"sheep ladders"—that were instantly spotted as she made her way along the mountain walls. Born with perfect coordination of eyes, legs, and muscles, Tor followed her with inborn confidence in his ability to go wherever she went. Leaping now from side to side along the front of a rock-faced wall, he landed on ledges no wider than one of his own tiny hoofs until he finally stood on a roughened incline below her. Here he looked into a densely wooded canyon where a creek ran through the tangled underbrush like a narrow cord of silver. At first he did not see any sign of life, but when he started up the cliff he caught sight of a mother fox and her young slipping out of the underbrush like soft, red shadows. They glanced at him, then vanished into the brush again. Curious, he waited for them to return. It was not until Tara gave an impatient bleat that he

hurried after her. When they reached the top of the cliff he was hungry, so his mother stopped long enough to let him nurse.

All through the days of his first summer Tor explored the country near the feeding areas until his mother's nervous bleats warned him to return. If he stayed away too long, she went searching for him, her calling sounds resembling the hoarse blasts of a foghorn. Gradually, though, he was allowed more freedom. He used this new independence to go farther away from the herd, becoming more and more curious about the world he lived in. One day, while nibbling on grass, he noticed a slight movement in a patch of brush nearby. A snowshoe rabbit, dressed in its summer coat of reddish-brown, was snipping off tender blades of grass inside the thicket. It came out and stared at Tor curiously for a few moments, then hopped off across the mesa. Once it stopped, stood up and scrubbed its face quickly with its fore paws, and went on again.

Tor was so interested that he followed. He could see it hopping along, and when the grass grew taller and thicker he hurried to catch up. He came upon it quite unexpectedly sitting on a hillock, this time washing its forepaws. It glanced at him, flipped its short, upturned tail, fluffy as a pom-pom, and darted through an opening in a pile of rocks. He sniffed around the jagged hole and tried to peek inside. Unable to see or smell the rabbit, he pawed the ground irritably. Finally growing tired of this one-sided game, he started back to his mother.

He had not gone far when he sensed he was lost. He tested the wind for a familiar scent, but at that moment the vague side-currents of air, eddying around the deep canyons and steep rim rocks, raced off in new directions, never reaching him. Confused and frightened, he began running around in circles, bleating at the top of his voice.

A hungry bobcat, slipping along underneath the rim of the cliff among the rocks and brush, heard him. At the first sound of Tor's frightened bleats, it moved to the top of the mesa with stealth and speed. Although there was not a sound from the bobcat's padded feet, instinct warned Tor that he was in danger. He stopped his bewildered circling long enough to sight a strange animal slinking across the mesa toward him. He had never seen a bobcat before, but its furtively moving body conveyed a deadly intent that filled him with terror. Bleating at the top of his voice again, he raced across the mesa in a confusion of zigzag motions that carried him over a bluff and down a steep hillside. Right behind was the bobcat, so absorbed in hooking Tor's hindquarters, it failed to notice the sudden appearance of Tara charging down from the rear—a mistake which allowed the cat only one startled glance in her direction before it was tossed into the air with a jarring butt. Yowling with fury, it landed on the rocky ground in an awkward sprawl, but jumped up quickly to fight. The bobcat's spitting and snarling was a danger signal that failed to stop Tara from ploughing down the hillside, wild-eyed with rage. Unnerved by so much power and anger headed in its direction, the bobcat leaped frantically backward and vanished over the mesa rim.

Tara sniffed Tor all over to see if he was hurt. Finding him unharmed, but still shaking with terror, she licked his face, making soft little bleating sounds as they nuzzled each other. He was safe. That was all she wanted. Giving a quick glance around, she led Tor back to the feeding grounds, stopping several times to nuzzle and lick his face, her warm tongue a caress that calmed his fears.

2. *Sharp Horns*

Tor soon forgot his frightening adventure. He was with his mother and the herd again, safe from the unexpected dangers of a strange, but exciting, new world.

The bighorns were taking their afternoon siesta. Some of the ewes were lying down scratching themselves. Their faded winter coats of grayish-white were beginning to shed and would soon turn into the rich brown they took on in August. Others were rubbing their chins on nearby rocks or nibbling on their legs and flanks. Now and then a ewe would get up and eat for a few minutes, then lie down again. The lambs would do the same. Wise One browsed on a grassy incline where she could watch over the little flock.

Toward evening the bighorns bedded down. Dusk settled into a night that was clear and cold. Only the faint scraping of loosened gravel rolling down the hillside broke the silence. The crescent moon, cradled lazily on the tip of a mountain peak, cast ghostly shadows of light over the crags where the wild sheep slept. It was their ancestors who had chosen a home range on the west slope of the Wind River Mountains, and their inherent clannish nature would continue to keep them in this selected area, unless unforeseeable forces of nature drove them off.

Tor, who had been dozing near his mother, suddenly stirred, as if startled. But the sound he had heard was only the wind blowing across the crags, rustling patches of dry brush, a delicate, crackling noise that he recognized. His small, pointed ears flicked back and forth straining to hear the faint and unfamiliar night-calls that had so often alerted his attention. But the air was filled with a great stillness, and he closed his eyes again, content with his mother's nearness.

Tor's strength and aggressive spirit soon made him the accepted leader of the lambs. He could run faster, leap higher, and butt harder than the others. Arn was Tor's ally and companion. When they weren't teasing Popo and Meta they were exploring the country together. But the day was never complete until all of them played their favorite game of trying to knock each other off cliffs and ledges. Swift and sure-footed, they ran around spiralling crags, dodging flank attacks and side-swiping hoofs, often landing on some tiny foothold their keen eyes had detected only seconds earlier.

The lambs spent most of their time near the rim rocks. Here they saw small rodents, but they had rarely seen birds on the barren crags until one morning a flock of mountain magpies flew over the sheep and settled on their backs. The birds pecked at the minute larvae they found in the heavy fleece of the bighorns, but the sheep never stopped feeding, never looked up, and did not shake themselves. Although the adult sheep seemed to enjoy having the birds peck them, Tor did not want a magpie on his back and shook it off. The bird flew over to Popo and began wiping its black bill along her neck. Cocking his head on one side Tor slipped up from behind and butted her. Startled, Popo jumped high, tossing the magpie from her back. It landed on the ground, wings fluttering angrily. Cawing shrilly, it swooped upward then dived straight down at Tor, its wings beating his face. Frightened, he swung about and ran, the black-and-white comet in swift pursuit, its sharp bill drilling his rump hard enough to make him leap in the air and bleat. He reached safety by diving

14

under his mother with a sliding butt that almost up-ended her. The magpie continued to fly around them, cawing angrily. Tor stayed close to his mother. He had had enough of feathery assaults!

The birds did not stay long, flying off in a sudden melodious flutter of white-patched, ebony-colored wings. Now Tor singled out Popo and Meta for a butting match. Arn joined in and the four of them pushed each other back and forth until they fell to their knees. Jumping up, they raced across the flat, and as Tor passed a ewe he accidently hit her rump. She wheeled and caught one of his hind legs on a horn, tossing him into a second ewe near him, who butted him hard enough to make him spin. Then Arn hit him. His hard little head caught Tor on one flank and rolled him under a third ewe. She kicked up her hind legs. her sharp hoofs giving him a broadside that made him grunt. Dizzy from so much butting and spinning, he made the first woolly object a target.

It happened to be Roc.

Tor hit the young ram a resounding whack.

Snorting with surprise and anger, Roc lifted Tor on his horns and bounced him against a pile of rocks. Tor lay quite still, the breath knocked out of him. Roc started for him again, but Tara moved in swiftly, lowering her head. Her action brought the young ram up short.

Tara licked Tor's face, but he was not seriously hurt. He got up and nuzzled his mother, the teasing mood shaken out of him. As he went off to play with the other lambs, he eyed Roc warily, his rump still smarting from the painful encounter with sharp horns and the pile of rocks.

The bighorns had been without salt all winter, and now their skins itched and their throats were dry. It was not until Wise

16

One felt a hotness in her own throat that she sensed the need of the herd and made her way down a side-ridge, the bighorns strung out in single file behind her. The old ewe seemed in no hurry. The sheep grazed along the way. Once they stopped and drank water trickling from a melting snow bank, licking their mouths afterwards with evident pleasure. They required little water and seldom went down to lower creek levels even in summer, since caches of snow were always available in the high Wind River Mountains. The lambs gathered around the older sheep and licked the snow, too, but they soon discovered it was more amusing to butt each other into it.

After the adult bighorns finished drinking and the lambs were chastened into obedience with a sharp nudge or two, Wise One led them to a lower plateau. Here they stopped and rested. Toward dusk they fed long and well, and then moved on to carefully chosen bed-grounds just under the crest of the ridge where possible enemies could be heard approaching from any direction. The nest-beds were circular hollows in the ground, formed by pawing and scraping away loose stones which would be uncomfortable to lie on. Like all nest-beds, they were used nightly when the sheep moved back and forth on their home range.

Next morning, before dawn, the sheep followed Wise One to the cliff side of the plateau where she stopped and looked into a canyon. They would have to go down a towering rock-faced wall, then cross a creek in order to reach the next ridge system. The canyon was deep and heavily fringed with willows, pines, and aspens. She knew bears, bobcats, and coyotes often lurked in these dense woods. As she started to make the first leap downward, she hesitated, having caught sight of movement below. The sheep crowded around her and saw a black bear and her two cubs coming out of a thicket near the stream. The cubs were wrestling playfully, but they stopped long enough to climb an aspen tree, slapping at each other all the way up the trunk. When they reached the top, down they came, tail first, falling the last few feet and landing on their haunches. Running over to their mother, they watched her rip open a rotten log, then joined her in sniffing and peering and scraping inside for ants, grubs, and honey. But when the mother did not find what she was looking for, she pushed aside the log rather petulantly and waddled up the hillside, followed by her playful cubs.

Wise One waited until their brown rumps disappeared over the horizon, then she took the first leap down the almost perpendicular wall. Tara followed, Tor behind her. Springing sideways from the ledge, he spread his feet out to brace himself, and with body parallel to the front of the cliff, landed on a bench of stone below, his muscles acting as brakes, his belly touching the surface. Leaping again, he hugged the wall more closely, controlling his half-falling, half-leaping movements by holding back with his cushioned hoofs on the small ledges. Down, down, down he went, and when he neared the bottom he leaped off into space with a spring that landed him on the ground and out of the way of the other bighorns, jumping one behind the other.

Wise One sniffed the air, her eyes probing the underbrush along the canyon walls. Then she forded the creek and headed into the dense grove of pine and aspen trees. Tor was excited. This was new country to him. Mysterious country. It even smelled different.

The bighorns stepped almost soundlessly on the forest duff as they walked through the canyon. The soft bark on the aspens was torn and bumpy with new and old claw marks of bears, horn-thrusts of wandering elk and deer, squirrel gnawings, and the borings of woodpeckers, testifying to the playfulness, anger, or storage requirements of the animals and birds.

Tor was alert to the sounds coming from the deeply-shadowed grove of trees and brush. The pine and aspen forest was filled with muted sounds of humming, buzzing, squeaking, and chirping. Lizzards ran up and down tree trunks. Here and there a bird whisked through the sky, perching in a pine tree long enough to share its spring song with the earth-bound. Red squirrels with white breasts, their olive-colored summer coats of pepper-and-salt becoming redder on the legs, feet, tail, and ears, raced up pine trees. Their shrill, almost rackety bird-like sounds informed the bighorns that they were intruders. The sheep ignored their sudden appearance and their scolding voices. Even the *rat-a-tat-tat* of a colorful hairy woodpecker boring into an old stump did not disturb them. Only the bears had held their attention, so Tor sensed they were dangerous.

Wise One followed the path the bears had taken to a level stretch of ground where they nibbled on clumps of white sage and flowers. Bed-grounds were nearby, and they spent the night on the ridge.

3. Dangerous Journey

Early next morning Wise One led the way down the mountain. The bighorns walked slowly, stopping often to scan the hills. Tor did not understand why they were so watchful, but since his mother appeared uneasy, too, he stayed near her.

The hills were bare of grass, the ground rocky and dry, but when the sheep crossed a little gulch, they stopped to nibble on wild parsnip growing around a water hole. Afterwards, Tor followed his mother up a slope to a bank of white-colored earth, where the sheep were now licking the ground. Curious, Tor tasted it. The briny, biting flavor made the saliva glands in his mouth respond instantly. He liked it, so he licked it a few times more, his tongue savoring the salty juices oozing around his lips. However, he soon lost interest in the salt lick and went off to play with the other lambs. It was not until he saw a pair of mule deer, each with two fawns, that he returned. The does were large, grayish-brown in color, and their tails were tipped with black. The fawns were brown and still covered with white spots. The deer went to the far side of the hill and licked the salty earth, stopping only long enough to stare at the bighorns.

Tor took a few steps in the direction of the fawns, shook his head, and pawed the ground playfully. All five little ones stood eyeing each other with lively interest, then the fawns made long, high jumps towards their mother—and peeked at Tor from under her flanks. Tor stepped closer, but when the mule deer snorted he backed up hastily.

Arn came leaping over a little bluff and bounced into him, and they took off across the hillside. They had not gone far when they met several elk cows and their calves. The cows had lingered in a little valley deep with new grass until after the birth of their calves. Now they were following a trail through bighorn range to their own summer feeding grounds somewhere high in the mountains. The cows were larger than the mule deer, and their long-legged calves were husky, too. One male calf stopped and looked at Tor as if interested in getting acquainted, then changed his mind and ran after his mother.

Tor followed the elk to the salt lick, where they ate the salty earth in great noisy gulps. He kept edging closer to the bull calf, his bright, friendly eyes inviting him to play. This time the calf was quick to accept and they nosed each other, then kicked up their heels and chased each other around the hillside.

The elk cows seemed in a hurry and soon left the salt lick, ending the short, playful interlude. Tor watched them until they disappeared; then he lay down beside his mother, bunting her with affectionate little nudges.

Toward afternoon the bighorns left the salt lick for their bed-grounds, and the mule deer moved out. Wise One stopped several times and, her ears flicking back and forth constantly, she scanned the surrounding country before going on.

Suddenly a terrified bleating broke the silence. Wise One sensed instantly what the sound meant, and with a warning bleat she headed for the rim rocks, the other bighorns right behind her. When they reached the upper level, they looked down and saw Arn and his mother running through a dry wash, four big shaggy coyotes chasing them. The sheep were fleeing toward the rim rocks, Arn in front, his mother in back, using her body to protect him. Fast as they were, the coyotes quickly overtook

them, fanning out in a half-circle and running in and out, slashing the ewe's flanks. Arn's mother tried to dodge their attacks with high, zigzagging leaps, but each time her hoofs hit the ground the coyotes were there to strike her, ripping strips of flesh from her rump, sides, and neck until she finally lay in a crumpled and lifeless heap.

Arn gave one terrified glance behind and streaked for a high, rocky bluff, a coyote on his heels. Before he could leap to higher ground it caught him with a shoulder blow that rolled him over. He jumped up and tried to run but was knocked down again. Instantly, long, yellow fangs clamped into his throat, crushing out his life, his last breath a smothered, gurgling bleat.

Tor, watching from the safety of the rim rocks, trembled so violently that Tara pressed against him, as if the touch of her warm body would comfort him. He could not take his eyes away from the dead ewe and her lamb, the coyotes still tearing ravenously at their bodies. As the sheep continued to move up higher, he kept looking back until his mother nudged his rump hard enough to make him jump—her way of impressing on him the results of being incautious. That night he cuddled even closer to her.

Next day, Wise One led the bighorns back to their home range. Although their first trip of the season to the salt lick had ended in tragedy, they would return again several times before summer was over because they needed the soil minerals to keep them healthy during winter.

Spring was the time of year when the Wind River Mountains looked like a tumbled sea of green mist rising into the sky, coolly beautiful, mysterious, and aloof, even forbidding, as if they welcomed only the perennial guests of nature.

Forage was abundant and the lambs grew fast. By fall they were two feet tall, weighed eighty pounds, and were old enough to be weaned. Although Tor had been getting nourishment from grass, flowers, and tender foliage, he was quick to resent any denial of milk. Each time his mother refused him, he pawed the ground and rolled his eyes, then pranced around and butted her rump.

Popo became Tor's new companion. Meta followed them wherever they went, peeking at them from behind rocks and brush piles and giving Tor a sly kick whenever he came close enough. Sometimes, quite unexpectedly, Popo joined Meta against him. This sudden change in her loyalty was confusing. But it was not until they sideswiped him with their sharp hoofs that he went after them angrily. When he tried to head them off by leaping over a little bluff, he saw his mistake in mid-air— Roc and Ute were sunning themselves underneath! He hit Roc with a thud that made him grunt, bounced off his back, and kept on running until he found his mother. Later, when he saw Roc staring angrily at him, he sensed it would be safer to stay near her.

Tor soon forgot about Roc. He was too busy playing with Popo and Meta. But Roc resented the lamb who had butted and jumped on him and watched for an opportunity to punish Tor. His first assault almost catapulted Tor into a canyon. Tor accepted the unnerving episode as only a game, but one too dangerous for him to play, and stayed out of Roc's way. Again he fed near his mother.

But with the happy forgetfulness of the young, Tor returned a few days later to the investigation of his fascinating homeland. The grass on the mesa and craggy hillsides was tall enough now to give him a pleasing sense of adventure when he walked

24

through it, especially when strange little mice scurried underneath. Sometimes they leaped right at his nose! How startled he pretended to be—kicking up his heels and running just for the sheer joy of feeling his body in lively motion. It was while he was gamboling on a rocky knoll that he saw a big ram on the opposite hillside. He was moving slowly across a level bench above, nibbling on patches of grass. Tor did not know that Big Chief was master of the herd nor that the first flurries of snow on the mountain peaks were a warning signal that led him to the lower levels, for soon it would be the rutting season when he must fight and defend his little band of ewes against strange rams. Big Chief was dark brown with a white rump patch, the blackish tail joined to the brown of the back by a long, dark stripe, cutting the rump patch in two. His snout had a small, naked place between the nostrils; his chin was without a beard; his hoofs were black. The insides of his legs, as well as the back of his forelegs, were white, with the under side a pale cream color. His massive horns were so heavy it seemed it must be difficult for him to hold up his head. There were many wrinkles in his horns, as well as a cross-ridge for each year of his ten years of life. His powerful, compact body stood outlined against a backdrop of brown, green, and purple mountain hues—a living statue, over three hundred pounds of strength and beauty.

Tor was drawn to the old ram, and after watching him for several minutes, he crossed a narrow draw to get closer. Something about the way Big Chief stood, head up, the sun glinting on his enormous horns, made him look too big, too unapproachable, too fierce. Tor flipped his short tail and ran back to the safety of a little ridge where he stood watching the old ram.

Each day Tor slipped away from his playmates and followed Big Chief to his feeding grounds. Bolder now, he grazed as close as he dared, watching the old ram when he lay down, taking the load from his neck by resting the tip of one great horn on the ground. Growing even more courageous, he leaped in the air and shook himself to attract further attention. Big Chief stared down at him, the great gold-colored eyes set in penetrating appraisal, then he looked off into the distance again, as if no longer interested in the lamb he had sired. Tor could not know their relationship, but somehow sensed that he had been noticed.

4. Winter

October was the month of shorter days, colder weather, and the ground was brittle with frost. Storms blew up quickly: the sky darkened, and great jagged streaks of lightning cut through the swirling clouds. Thunder boomed overhead. At first the loud claps startled Tor, but when his mother continued to feed, he learned they were not to be feared.

With the coming of the first heavy snow storm, Wise One led the sheep to a cave in the rocks. They did not go far inside, only deep enough to find temporary shelter from the freezing winds. All of the bighorns crowded inside for their rest period except Big Chief. He stood on a lookout point, seemingly indifferent to the icy winds whipping his big body.

The sheep stayed in the cave until they grew hungry, then they went out to graze. During the feeding hours they never minded the weather. The frowzy baby coats of the lambs had been shed. Their winter pelage was an outercoat of dense, coarse hair, nearly three inches long, with a wool undercoat, which protected them from the iciest winds, the heaviest snow fall.

As the storms increased, the bighorns moved down from the higher slopes to a lower area on the same mountain, feeding along the ridges where the snow was light and grass and roots easy to get at. Wise One was forced to move about constantly, seeking lower levels for daily forage. As usual she set the pace through the snow, jumping up and forward, landing several feet ahead with each leap. The bighorns used her tracks, following in single file behind. The lambs soon grew tired, for they were young and inexperienced, but their mothers would not let them rest. Deep snow was dangerous for bighorns. It could prove to be a trap.

Tor learned that traveling up and down and across icy ledges could be tiresome and dangerous, too. Sure-footed as he was, he sensed the change in body and muscle action when walking over ice. Only once did he go spinning down a long, icy slope toward a hundred foot drop-off, stopping just short of the edge of the cliff when he rolled into a boulder. The impact skinned his face and forelegs and knocked the breath out of him. He got up slowly, warily, and looked at his mother, who was already on her way down to him. She stood by his side until his confidence returned; then they went up the slope together. After they reached the top, she gave him a sharp bunt, her fears now tempered with anger, warning him that he must be more alert to danger.

Although the mountains were covered with snow, and apparently deserted, many inhabitants of the cold, white world were moving about, some openly, others slyly, following the pattern of their lives. Tor saw coyotes nearly every day, their lean, shaggy bodies standing motionless in the underbrush. At night their eerie, complaining voices drifted across the canyons with rising notes of sharpness that seemed forced from the depths of empty bellies. Tor reacted instinctively and shivered. Small bands of snowshoe rabbits quite often fed in the ravines, snipping off every twig they could find with their slanted bite. They went from bush to bush stripping off the twigs within reach, then seeking out mounds of snow to lift them higher and higher so they could get to the lower branches of the trees. Their long, furry toes, or "snowshoes," were spread even wider in winter—

28

nature's way of protecting them from slipping on icy crusts or sinking into soft snow, where they would be at the mercy of predators.

As the bighorns walked along the edge of a high bluff, Wise One suddenly leaped into a huge snow drift pitched at a steep angle and slid down it, snow streaming over both shoulders. When it seemed as if she would surely fall into the canyon below, she braked her forelegs, whirled about, and galloped to the top.

The sheep crowded around her and lined up eagerly, ready to play this exciting game. As Tor waited his turn, Roc stepped in behind, head down. Tara rushed up and shoved him aside. For one moment he looked as if he might horn her, but turned away, blowing softly through his nostrils.

Tor peeked at Roc from behind his mother. Instinct warned him that this time the young ram had not been playing a game. Roc had intended to butt him into the canyon. Moving closer to his mother, Tor eyed the ill-tempered ram. From now on he would not trust this member of the herd.

Big Chief lay on a crag watching the sheep playing the snow game, but he was alert to any movement on the hills around him. Later, the bighorns bedded down in a sheltered nook where they could see the sun rise and feel its warmth.

November was the beginning of the rutting season. Although Roc and Ute were not yet three years old, the gradual change in their bodies from young rams to adult rams made them restless and quarrelsome. Soon they were fighting each other in earnest, as if they intended to mate. But Big Chief put a stop to this. When he shook his head and stomped one forefoot, they quieted down, not yet old enough or brave enough to fight him.

One morning a newcomer walked across a flat where the ewes

were feeding, carrying his curly horns with pride. Now, once again, Big Chief had to prove himself master of his flock. He stepped forward to meet the interloper. They stood side by side, at first nudging one another with their horns, then jabbing and raking each other's shoulders with their front hoofs, almost growling out their grunts. Suddenly they backed off for several feet and stood on their hind hoofs. Almost erect, they faced each other, then dropped to all fours and charged over the ground, meeting head-on, the crack of their horns shattering the mountain stillness. Big Chief's horns ripped into his opponent's shoulder drawing blood. Snorting again, they backed up and charged. This time they battered each other with such force that both rams reeled and staggered. Sides heaving, they stood quietly for several minutes, then lunged forward, sideswiping each other with their sharp hoofs. As they backed off for another encounter, the strange ram suddenly turned and trotted away.

Tor, who had been watching from a safe retreat, pawed the ground excitedly and butted at an imaginary opponent. When he saw Meta and Popo on a little ridge, looking down with nervous interest, he dashed toward them. They met him halfway down the slope in a real head-on butting match, a lively romp that soon tired the three of them, and they flopped to the ground.

During the mating season the lambs stayed out of Big Chief's way. His warlike restless energy frightened them. Nor did they go near their mothers, sensing that the big ram would take offense. He was not only master and protector of the flock but a mate to all of the breeding ewes and father to all of the lambs.

It was not until mid-January that all was quiet again, and Wise One led the sheep to the feeding grounds.

30

The weather was still bitterly cold. The raging winds seemed to have wrapped spring in their turbulent folds and blown away with it. Snow swirled thickly like a heavy fog. Sometimes several inches settled on the ground, and the bighorns pawed through it to reach the short, tender blades of grass and mountain clover underneath.

Big Chief began to feed farther away from the herd. Tor noticed that Roc and Ute were daily companions. Finally the three rams separated themselves entirely from the ewe-band. Tor was curious as to where they were going and followed, but when Big Chief snorted his disapproval he turned back hurriedly. Tor did not sense that Roc and Ute were now old enough to go with Big Chief. They had been taken into the ram clique by the leader.

As Tor started back to the herd, he saw a young male, or dog, fox peeking at him from behind a rocky knoll. He had seen an animal like this once before in the canyon. Knowing instinctively it would not hurt him, he watched the fox leave his hiding place and walk toward him.

Tor went to meet him. After they had sniffed each other cautiously, the fox gave a short bark, shook his bushy tail, and ran around Tor. Ready for a game, Tor kicked up his hind legs and took off across the snow-powdered mesa, the fox right behind, now and then nipping Tor's short tail. Tor did not appreciate the tail-nipping and whirled to butt the fox as the fox leaped, and they came together, head-on. Down went the fox and rolled over, but he was up quickly, staring at Tor in dazed surprise. Tor stared back. The little fox shook his head several times, as if to clear it, then trotted over to Tor and bunted him playfully. Tor let out a happy bleat and the two of them lay down side by side. The fox made a *chur-churring* sound of contentment and rubbed his nose against Tor's face. When a cold wind came up, the little fox flipped his bushy tail around his legs and peeked at Tor through the furry muff. As Tor reached out to nuzzle him, the fox suddenly began yapping with excitement, leaped to his feet, and ran after several mice just emerging from under the snow. Tor had seen mice several times before, but he had never chased them. He walked around while waiting for the little fox, but when the sky began to darken and his new friend did not reappear, he went back to the herd.

Tor met the little fox again several times. The fox delighted in nipping Tor's face, but when Tor playfully butted his small rump in return, he snapped back in annoyance. It was only when Tor went leaping wildly up and down the dangerous crags in a game of follow-the-leader, bighorn fashion, that their unusual friendship came to an end. The fox crouched on the cliff above and peeked down at Tor. He could not join his playmate in this fantastic game, and so he trotted off across the mesa. Tor watched the fox until he disappeared, then returned to the feeding grounds, and once again Popo and Meta became his companions.

5. A New Order

During the winter the bighorns left their nest-beds from one to three hours later in the day. On their way down a chasm, ice was hanging from the rocks and bushes. A ptarmigan in her winter plumage of white, only her tail feathers and black beak showing against the snow, stopped scratching under a ledge-rock long enough to pull tiny globules of frozen mud from between her toe feathers. Then she walked up a little rise and disappeared through a crevice in a rock.

Wise One was in the lead, with Tara and the other bighorns strung out behind her. The sheep leaped from boulder to boulder, stoping briefly to paw under protected dirt ledges for grass. When they had gone halfway down the chasm, a loud rumbling startled them. The bighorns sensed instantly what the sound meant and bounded up the nearest incline just as the snow began cascading over the opposite cliff. Roaring and booming, tons of rocks and snow crashed down into the canyon. As the sheep stood looking, a heavy mist of fine snow rose in billowing clouds from below, drifting slowly upward and over the mountain.

Wise One had been under the opposite cliff and had caught the full force of the avalanche.

When the noise abated, the bighorns milled around nervously, then walked back to the edge of the cliff and stared into the chasm, searching through the still rising mist of snow for Wise One. Tara was the first to turn away. Accepting the old ewe's death, she started along the ridge ahead of the other sheep, as if she had appointed herself the new leader. But an older ewe did not agree. She challenged Tara with a butt from the rear that sent her reeling. Tara quickly regained her balance and with an indignant snort turned to charge her opponent head-on. They butted and knocked each other about, moving along the cliff's edge, their sharp horns ripping into each other. With head pushing against head, Tara finally shoved the older ewe into a snow drift, where she teetered percariously on the rim of the cliff before leaping back to safety. Tara stared at the other ewes, and when there were no more challenges she stepped briskly across the ridge and down a lower level, the others following behind her.

The winter days passed slowly. By the latter part of May tiny horns had sprouted from Popo and Meta's foreheads. Tor's were longer and quite heavy at the base. The horns and the sparse, long hairs growing between their ears gave the lambs an untidy look about the head, adding a touch of clownish gaiety to their appearance.

Tor had not yet outgrown a close relationship with his mother. For a year now he had been the center of her attention and affections, so when he saw her fondle Bow, a new-born lamb, he was disturbed. He had followed her to a brush-covered ledge and there it was, standing on wobbly legs looking up at him. Tor threw up his head and backed away. Although his mother bleated a gentle welcome, he turned, jumped on a ledge above her bed, and peered down at her and the baby lamb. Again she bleated, a coaxing bleat that was repeated several times before he finally joined her. After sniffing the lambs' cold little nose with increasing interest he returned to the feeding grounds above.

Restless, he went to the high rock-faced cliff the bighorns

used as a trail to the next ridge system and the salt lick. Suddenly a squirrel ran along a lower ledge, its usual rackety, birdlike voice raised in squeaks of alarm. Instantly curious, Tor leaped downward. His hoofs had barely touched the ledge when he heard the whirr and whistle of wings. He was struck on the head with such force he was almost knocked into the canyon. As the Golden Eagle came at him again, he threw his body sideways and jumped off the ledge. The eagle hovered over him in a feathery cloud of raucous terror all the way down to a jagged rock Tor had sighted in mid-air. He dodged its razor-sharp beak and striking talons by leaping into a brush-covered ledge that jutted out from the canyon wall. Here he watched the eagle until it finally spiralled into the sky, its shrill, eerie screams smothered in a lazy drift of puffy white clouds.

Shaken by his encounter with the eagle, Tor's first instinct was to return to his mother, but after hesitating a moment he continued down the cliff, now and then casting wary glances at the sky. The creek was knee-deep and he forded it, stopping once to take a long, cool drink as he searched the trees and brush. The canyon was familiar country. He need not be afraid. Moving forward, he rubbed his shoulder and rump against an aspen tree, emitting soft little groans of pleasure, his small, pointed ears flicking back and forth to catch the faintest sounds. Clumps of flowers were growing on a bank high above—tantalizing tidbits for a hungry lamb. Hearing a rustling sound, he glanced quickly behind him, but it was only red squirrels running through dry leaves. The air was warm; the willows had the odor of dampness about them. He nibbled on a few leaves, his body crushing brittle ends of twigs as he walked along. He stopped and sniffed the air currents, but the cliff walls were so high they shut off any odor from above. Only the moist, humid air of the canyon warmed his nostrils.

Step by step he made his way up the bank, his mouth filling with saliva at the expected tastiness of the flowers. They were almost within reach when a crashing sound made him whirl about. Breaking cover was a bear—and it was headed up the bank toward him!

Tor let out a gasping sneeze of terror and leaped over the top of the bear, landing a few feet away. There was little distance between them as they ripped through thickets of willows and sagebrush, on through a grove of trees and across the creek, spraying geysers of water in all directions. Tor reached the cliff first and jumped. The bear, seconds behind, slapped at him, the tip of its knifelike claws beading his rump with blood. The sudden shock of pain sickened Tor, and he teetered on a narrow ledge. As the bear reached for him again, he jumped, and he kept on jumping until he was out of danger. With heart pounding and nostrils flared, he stopped and looked back. The bear was sliding down the rough wall, tail first, scattering pebbles as its claws hooked into the granite surface. Tor's rump pained him, and by now his hind legs were beginning to feel stiff. Aware that a misstep would mean death in the canyon, he started up the cliff again, each painful leap taking him higher and higher until he reached the top, two thousand feet up.

Tor hobbled back to the ledge overlooking his mother's bed. Tara, who had been feeding a short distance away, saw him and followed quickly. She began licking his torn flesh, the soothing touch of her warm tongue making him feel safe again.

The following summer, when Tor was two years old, he was nearly as tall as his mother, and his horns resembled those of an adult ewe. By the time he was three years old, he weighed a hundred and seventy pounds, with horns that were beginning

to sweep back and up in what would one day be the massive curls of an adult ram. The gradual change in his size made him less afraid of Roc, but he still did not trust the older ram, sensing a controlled hate in him that was violent enough to kill.

The social structure of the herd had gradually changed, too. Tor was now entirely independent of his mother, and Popo and Meta were no longer his playmates. He was an adult ram, and they were adult ewes, and this separated them, except during the rutting season. Now Tor turned to Bow for companionship. The younger ram enjoyed Tor's attention and tried to lick his face at every opportunity. Tor would have horned any other ram who tried to do this, but not Bow. He had a special affection for the younger ram.

Big Chief had continued to follow the usual pattern of his life, returning to the ewe band during the rutting months and chasing Ute and Roc out of the herd. Here he was master. It was not until February that they joined him again and the three went off together.

Usually Tor would not see them again until the first sharp winds of early fall, but when the June sun began to melt the snow on the higher hills and color the earth with grass and flowers, Big Chief returned. He bunted Tor, indicating that Tor was to follow him. Tor could not know that the years lay heavy on Big Chief's aging body; his sight was dimming. Nor could he know that Big Chief had chosen to train him to be his future protector, as old rams often did.

Tor learned that the country where the old ram had gone after the rutting season was neither mysterious nor far away. He had only followed familiar and deeply-gutted hoof trails in a different area of their home range. Roc and Ute were waiting for them. Roc turned his back on Tor, one hind leg jerking nervously—a sure sign that Tor's presence was unwelcome and difficult to accept.

The rams fed on the higher hills for several days, then gradually worked along the ridges to their twelve-thousand-foot-high summer retreat in the Wind River Mountains on the west slope of the Continental Divide. Here they found various kinds of plants and grass in narrow draws: lichens in rocky swales; alpine flowers, too, their delicate flavor always a delight to their tongues and a sweetness in their bellies.

Tor's close companionship with Big Chief was an exciting experience. He soon learned he was to act as sentinel and scan the country while the other rams lay in the customary crouch of a rabbit, resting and dozing. During the day he seldom lay down, and even when he did he was constantly testing the wind and peering about, watching for animals he had learned to fear. It was not until early September that he saw strange figures walking along a flat below. Their movements were unlike those of animals, and he snorted to attract Big Chief's attention. Big Chief got up, took one look, and reacted instantly to the moving figures that were their human enemies. Giving the half-snorting, half-sneezing sound of danger, they wheeled about at his command and ran just as a bullet *pinged* into a gravel bank near them. Big Chief did not stop running until he found a more remote feeding area. Even then he looked cautiously around and over little rocky points to see if they were being followed. Tor sensed that the *pinging* sound had been connected in some way with the strange, moving figures and that it was dangerous.

6.   The Hunters

Tor and Big Chief bedded near one another and quite often fed side by side. The old ram followed trustfully a few feet behind Tor, as they climbed pinnacles of dizzy heights and trotted along sheer, rock-faced mountain walls where a misstep would mean a fall of several thousand feet.

Ute appeared indifferent to Tor's presence, but Roc's hostility was roused again. Resentful of Big Chief's choice of Tor as his companion, he watched for an opportunity to kick the younger ram over a cliff. It came one day when Tor was standing guard on a lookout point. Roc slipped up behind, ready to butt him into the canyon, but the crack of gravel alerted Tor and he leaped to one side, avoiding the savage attack. After that, he tried to stay closer to Big Chief, sensing the old ram would horn Roc if he attempted to hurt him.

The rams did not leave their summer feeding grounds until after the first snowfall. When the storm was over, the sun shone palely, but not enough to warm the chill in the air. The rams stopped to feed, then rested on jutting rocks, watching the country around them.

Big Chief seemed in no hurry to join the ewes. Each rest period stretched out well beyond the usual hours of feeding and scratching. Roc's temper began to rise. He wanted to be on the move and paced the ground with increasing restlessness, even starting down a trail, but when Big Chief turned and stared at him he came back. He dared not go off ahead of the old ram.

42

Although he was impatient, he was not yet strong enough to wrest the leadership from him by force.

Big Chief continued to be annoyingly unconcerned. Even Ute grew restless, but Tor restrained his impatience. He was enjoying the companionship of the old ram too much.

A few days later Big Chief indicated that he was ready to resume their journey by first going to a rocky ledge and scanning the country. He stood there a long time, as if mentally photographing every inch of the grandeur of his home range—the rugged mountains, where from birth he had fed, mated and fought. Then he turned slowly and walked down the trail.

Lying concealed in a thick covert of brush and pines was a hunter. Accompanying him was the guide required by state law for non-residents hunting game in a national forest, national park, or federal game refuge. The hunter had been congratulating himself that his name had come up in the Annual Wyoming Bighorn Sheep Drawing. Now he would be allowed to hunt legally. There was a bag limit of one mature ram, having at least three-quarter curl horns, and when he saw Big Chief he could hardly keep from shouting. What a beauty! His days of rugged scouting in the sleet and snow had finally paid off. He did not want to miss getting the most beautiful ram he had ever seen.

"Look how smart he is!" he whispered to his Indian guide. "He's walking along the under section of the ridge instead of against the skyline."

The eyes of the Indian guide were sad. Twice before he had seen this huge ram standing on a pinnacle like the topmost star on a granite Christmas tree, inaccessible, breathtaking! He could not say to this stranger: "Please do not kill this ram. He is too noble. He should die here, in his own way, not by the hand of man, without a chance to defend himself." But the horns were trophies of a lifetime no hunter would forego. If only the cold side-currents of air, eddying around the jagged peaks and steep rim rocks, would carry their scent to the old ram!

As Big Chief moved leisurely down the mountain, the hunter watched him through his binoculars. "Twelve rings, maybe thirteen," he said, turning to his guide. "I can't be sure. I *can* be sure of one thing, though. I'll be doing him a service, as well as myself. Coyotes or cougars will be pulling him down one of these days, or he will die of starvation. I'll bet his teeth are worn to the gums."

The Indian guide admitted that to himself. The ram would not live much longer. He had been a wise old ram to live this long with legal and illegal hunters searching for trophy game. But he should die as he had lived, boldly, fiercely, making his animal enemies pay for his death.

The hunter's eyes followed Big Chief as he came toward them. "If that young ram would only get out of the way!" he whispered irritably, for now Tor was walking near the old ram. The hunter had barely finished speaking when Tor suddenly froze, sensing danger. At that moment Big Chief turned. Head up, he stood facing death, unaware that the hand on the trigger trembled for an instant. Then the hunter fired, and Big Chief went down, killed instantly.

At the sound of the shot Roc and Ute fled in terrified confusion, not knowing from which direction it had come. Tor ran, too, then stopped suddenly and glanced back at Big Chief lying motionless an the ground. It was not until he saw the two-legged creatures coming toward him that, sensing his own danger, he topped the ridge with a speed that made the hunter laugh heartily. "I'll bet it's the first time that young ram ever

44

saw a man or heard a gun," he said, still laughing. "He's learned a lesson he will never forget."

The Indian guide silently agreed.

Tor returned to the herd, stirred by the memory of Big Chief lying on the hillside, his head at a twisted angle, the tip of one great curled horn buried in the snow-covered earth. The icy blackness of the night sent a chill from his nose to his tail. He walked about until the silence of the world around him calmed his fears; then he lay down.

Next morning, when the sun rose dimly in a slate-blue sky, Tor returned to the ridge where Big Chief had been killed, but he could not find him. He kept following the deeply gutted trails, criss-crossing them again and again. When he reached the ridge to the north, he walked more slowly, as if every foot of ground might yield a clue to Big Chief's disappearance. He stopped and sniffed the ground, then the air, his nose exploring a sudden icy wind. Although he sensed that the search was useless, he went on, following the ridge to its summit. Looking down he saw a band of coyotes trotting toward a little canyon. Their moving bodies held his eyes for a few minutes, then he hurried down the trail, careful to avoid timbered draws and shadowed swales where coyotes often lay in wait. He reached the feeding grounds and saw Roc and Ute lying on a knoll watching him. As he stood looking at them, gaging his future with the older rams, Roc got up, eyes flashing with anger. Tor understood. Roc would never allow him to be a member of the ram clique. Too old to stay with the ewes and lambs, he accepted Bow's company again, and they fed and bedded near each other.

In the days that followed, Tor could see Roc and Ute's concern with each other. The herd must have a new master, one to be chosen either by consent or combat. Each day Roc and Ute grew more short-tempered. Wherever one went the other was right behind. If Ute was in the lead, Roc caught up and walked a few steps ahead. If Roc was in the lead, Ute did the same; then they would stop and stare at each other. Ute furnished the spark that set them off when he accidently stumbled into Roc, one horn jabbing Roc's side. Both rams turned at the same instant and stood on their hind hoofs, then suddenly dropped to all fours and charged. The impact made Ute spin and reel and Roc stagger and fall, but Roc leaped up and they charged again. This time the force of the blow crumpled Ute's fore legs. He tried to jump up, but Roc lunged at him, striking his shoulder, knocking him all the way to the ground. Before Ute could rise Roc struck him again, opening a deep gash on his shoulder. As Roc backed off, forefeet raised, body poised for another powerful drive, Tor moved in unexpectedly and hit the older ram with all of the strength he possessed, spinning Roc around. The spin caught Tor on the rebound with a blow below the heavy base of his horns, making the blood gush from his nose. Dazed, Tor took charge after charge, head-on, sideways to shoulder and rump, until he was wobbling on his feet, blood streaming from his ears, nose, shoulders and flanks. Roc showed no mercy. He was doing something he had always wanted to do and followed up each charge with another more violent until Tor was knocked unconscious. Roc moved toward him again, as if for a final blow, but Ute shoved him back with such force that he almost fell. Roc snorted and walked away, an ugly gleam in his eyes.

It was several minutes before Tor opened his eyes. Raising his head briefly he dropped it, as if it were too heavy to hold up. Finally forcing himself to his feet, he limped to his bed-grounds, Bow following. It was not until the next day that he went out on the mesa to feed.

7.   A Decision

Tor's dislike of Roc was now always with him, but he refused to leave the herd. He found shelter in the mouth of a little cave, his ears pricking to attention as he listened to branches of dry brush rasp back and forth in the wind. Bow lay beside him, gently licking the open wounds on his body.

As the days passed from September into late October, storms were more frequent and deep snow covered the mountains. Freezing winds blew down from the crags, swirling heavy black clouds that burst over the hills in thunderous torrents of rain, rolling boulders into the canyons.

Tor was now three-and-a-half years old, ready to mate. He was restless, irritable, no longer content to be companionable with Bow, and walked the hills constantly, his eyes following the older rams and the ewes.

During the first days of the rutting season Roc took over the flock of ewes. Ute challenged him and they fought, but this time the battle did not last long. Somehow they seemed to have come to an agreement, and Roc allowed Ute to mate within the herd.

Tor stayed on the outer fringe of the ewe-band and followed Popo constantly. His sly mating attempts so infuriated the older rams, they joined forces to fight him. Their united attacks finally drove him out of the herd. Although he was reluctant to leave, he sensed Roc would continue to punish him unmercifully, and he was not yet big enough nor strong enough to protect himself.

After leaving the herd, Tor followed side-ridges and open

flats where the fury of the winds kept the snow from packing. He covered more than twenty miles of rough mountain terrain before he saw ewes on a side-hill pawing for grass under the snow. Standing on a pile of rocks nearby was a ram.

Tor, excited by the ewe scent, curled back his upper lip. The mating instinct made him feel as big and powerful as his adversary. Confident, unafraid, his neck muscles began to swell. He took a few steps up the hill and walked toward the ewes—a signal that alerted the ram. Down he came and Tor went to meet him; the customary ritual of shoulder-jabbing was quickly followed by a head-on collision that lifted Tor off his feet. Backing up and wheeling, he met the second charge, which cracked his skull with such force that he could hardly see. The ram started after him again, but this time he retreated, and the ram did not follow.

The next day, and for several days after that, Tor tried to enter the band, but he was always driven off. He refused to leave, patiently waiting for an opportunity to outmaneuver the ram.

One morning he saw the ewes on a slope not too far away. They were alone. Slipping along a trail that led to the opposite slope, he rounded a rocky point. The ram was waiting for him. Charging, he felled Tor with a body blow that knocked him to the edge of the cliff. The ram followed up his assault and butted Tor again. Tor rolled over the cliff, landing on a wide ledge several feet below, where he lay partly stunned. The ram stared down at him. After a short, disdainful snort, he went back to his ewes.

Snow began falling and a cave, opening off the ledge, offered protection. Tor got up and went inside. He lay down and licked the bruised and swelling flesh on his forelegs, so engrossed that it was several minutes before a strange odor in the cave piqued his curiosity. He did not know it was the scent of a cougar. Feeling uneasy, he got up and sniffed the floor and the walls of the cave, then he stepped outside and breathed deep of the icy air, trying to catch the unfamiliar smell from different directions. When it eluded him, he went inside and lay down, but he remained restless, getting up every few minutes to check the walls of the cave and test the air outside.

Early next morning he left the cave, limping up a narrow trail that wound across the front of the cliff to the mesa above, stopping once to lick the bruises on his forelegs. By now several inches of snow covered the hills, so he walked through a sparse growth of pines and brush on the mesa where the country was more open. Although his view was clear, he stopped often, sniffing, listening, scanning the distant hillsides and draws.

Suddenly he became uneasy. He stood still for several moments, his nose exploring the air, then went on.

A few minutes later he stopped again and stared intently at the brush and trees fringing the mesa. A faint shadow seemed to move behind a heavy outgrowth of trees and brush not too far away. He watched it closely, and when it did not move again he went on. He walked a short distance, stopped and looked back, then took a few more steps forward. Suddenly there was that strange odor again. Sniffing the air he turned about, and there was the shadow, moving toward him in great leaps!

Tor headed for the cliff side of the mesa again, too frightened to feel any stiffness or pain in his forelegs. The cougar, wise and swift, bounded straight across the snowy ground, cutting off his retreat, forcing him to run downhill—a cougar's way of catching bighorns.

The hunter and the hunted raced along the mesa, leaping over logs, jumping from one incline to another, feathering the snow as their feet cracked against dry wood underneath. The cougar's tremendous leaps kept it only a few feet behind Tor, its lithe body stretched out in a desperate attempt to hook its claws into his hindquarters. Gathering speed, the cougar threw its body into another mighty leap, landing close enough to make Tor lunge to one side. Its huge paw struck at air. Wild-eyed, Tor again streaked for the cliff, the cougar right behind him, but this time he was not fast enough to catch Tor before he plunged a hundred feet down the front of the cliff, his cushioned hoofs controlling the velocity of his fall by striking little ledges and roughened inclines. His body whipped back and forth in half-falling, half-leaping movements. When Tor reached bottom, he crossed the ravine and bounded up the opposite cliff to the top, never stopping to look back.

The cougar eyed Tor's vanishing white rump with a low, snarling growl. Having missed its quarry, it sniffed the air, looked around, yawned, blinked its eyes sleepily, then walked along the edge of the cliff, the dark brown tip of its long tail twitching.

Tor's belly finally stopped its convulsive churning and his wildly beating heart quieted. Yet with nostrils flared and head jerking nervously, he continued to search the snow-covered hill-sides for a glimpse of the cougar. He had never seen an animal like it before, and had just learned that bears and coyotes were not his only enemies. After carefully searching the brushy draws, he was satisfied that the cougar was not hiding nearby, and went on again.

Tor followed a treeless ridge for several miles, until his power-ful eyes caught sight of five young rams his own age on a lower slope. They, too, were searching for ewe bands. Filled with the

violent energy of the mating season, they were taking time out to fight each other as they roamed the hills.

As soon as Tor joined them he was challenged. The first battle was so stimulating that he decided to stay with them, fighting each ram before he was accepted into the group. A month of lively jousts taught him how strong he was, knowledge that added to his self-confidence. After a few weeks of rigorous battles that netted only unsuccessful mating attempts, he again chose to wander alone. He met "hermit" rams, who for some reason known only to themselves, refused to conform to herd rules and lived mainly alone. Each one was quick to let him know that he was intruding on private territory. He did not challenge them.

After one such encounter, he followed a trail that led across a gully and up a wooded hillside pocket. As he walked leisurely along the trail, scanning the country around him, sniffing the air for the scent of ewes, he saw a buck mule deer across a little canyon. It was walking along the base of a ledge broken by fissures when the soft, brownish-gray body of a cougar suddenly shot out of a cave above and landed on its back. With one lightning movement of a big paw the cougar reached for the deer's muzzle and jerked back its head, snapping the neck bones. The buck collapsed. The cougar, having learned how to kill antlered prey, lay down beside it, forepaws pressed against the deer's neck, then sank its teeth into the jugular vein.

Tor hid behind a thick grove of young spruce trees and watched the cougar. Overcome by a sickening fear, he turned and hurried along the ridge, bedding down miles away before nightfall.

Tor continued his search for ewes, following side-ridges where brush and trees were sparse and snow lay on the ground in a

54

thin, pebbled carpet. Gradually, the driving urge to seek ewes and fight rams lessened. As he lay in a newly-made bed, he watched the pale moon shadows slide over the snowy hillsides. The trees were tall, fringed spears of white against the starry sky. The snow-capped mountain brush sprawled in grotesque mounds, as if in forced acceptance of a winter gift too heavy to enjoy. Feeling a sudden loneliness, he got up and walked around.

The next day he started back to his herd, but soon he stopped. He stood looking at the distant hills of his home range, his clannish nature urging him to return. But the rutting season had given him a taste of freedom that he liked. It beckoned him to new pastures and new ways of life—without Roc and Ute. Holding his head high, he smelled the almost freezing air. Suddenly he made a strange half-snorting, half-coughing sound. He turned quickly away from the direction of his herd and back-tracked the ridge. The hills ahead, as yet unexplored, drew him like a magnet.

8. *Destiny*

At last the shifting winds brought traces of warmth to the cold blackness of an early morning in April. By late afternoon the snow was soggy, the air misty with moisture. In a few days many ridges and south-facing mountain shoulders were bare. At last the hills were green again, flowers were in bloom, and the waterways free of ice.

Tor wandered from one mountain range to another, meeting lone rams like himself, fighting when necessary, acquiring respect from his opponents that gradually turned into friendships. Later these rams became the nucleus of a band willing to accept him as their leader.

During summer he took his companions to the mountain peaks above Green River Lakes. Here they lolled in lazy good humor, now and then testing the strength of their bodies and horns in playful bouts.

In November, though, their complacence was replaced by dangerous mating battles with each other, but never with Tor. He was the recognized leader of power and authority, and they left him to his conquests. After the rutting season they followed him to the lower hills. Lame, scarred and lethargic, they fed on the rich, succulent clusters of bunch grass which helped to restore their energy. The rams that had stayed with Tor through the summer and the rutting season now went their separate ways and he was alone once more. He continued to wander, obedient only to the demands of each day, content, not yet ready to return to his own herd. As the months passed he grew big and handsome, a dangerous six-year-old ram, weighing three hundred pounds, with grayish-brown horns that curled in more than a three-quarter circle.

It was not until the following summer that he turned his footsteps in the direction of the old feeding grounds where he had first gone with Big Chief. He saw Roc and Ute on a craggy point watching him, but he did not stop his upward climb. That evening he lay where he had a clear view of the surrounding country, his summer coat glowing a soft, brownish-gray in the fading sunlight, his luminous eyes searching the mountains with minute care. He settled himself more comfortably in his nest-bed, forelegs tucked under him, ears flicking to the whispers of sound around him.

During the summer Tor walked the trails and climbed the pinnacles he and Big Chief had walked and climbed together. He saw Roc and Ute every day, but he took little interest in their presence, perhaps not wanting to renew old feuds. Occasionally he caught glimpses of a ewe-band feeding on the hillsides below, recognizing them as his own. His curiosity was stirred, but he remained aloof. Quite often he fed and bedded where he could look down on Roc and Ute, a lofty attitude that began to edge Roc's temper. But it was not until after an early snowfall that he openly challenged Tor. He sensed that Tor meant to return to the ewe-band and he would fight to kill!

Tor understood. With eyes flashing and mane erect, he went to meet Roc. Their first sharp, challenging neck-jabs were soon spent and they backed up, stood on their hind hoofs and catapulted themselves straight as an arrow at each other. The impact made them stagger and reel. Shaking their heads, they backed

off for another encounter, reared up, then lowered their heads and charged. This time each ram tried to rip his opponent's shoulder or back with the tips of his big horns. When both missed, they stared at each other, grunted, and ground their teeth. Lowering their heads again, they came together with such force that they sent each other staggering for several feet. Dazed with the impact, they stood with open jaws and half-closed eyes for several minutes, then they attacked again. This time they struck each other sideways and upward with their sharp hoofs, cutting long gashes. First backing away, they turned and rushed forward. They met, horns locking, necks twisting almost to the breaking point before they separated. They charged half a dozen times more, their massive horns coming together with a shock that seemed powerful enough to grind them to splinters. But they only reeled and shook their heads, then slowly backed off, snorting, groaning, and pawing the ground in their rage. Bleeding profusely at nose and ears, and apparently suffering great pain, they continued to fight, the sound of their battering horns as sharp as rifle shots.

It was not until Tor neared the brink of a cliff, his hind hoofs tumbling a pile of loose stones into the canyon below with a roaring clatter, that he sensed his danger and leaped forward just as Roc charged. They came together with a sledge-hammer blow that up-ended Roc on the hillside and sent Tor whirling in dizzying circles. Regaining his balance, he started for Roc, but the older ram was stretched out, unconscious. With a short, disdainful grunt, Tor walked away, head up, but swaying groggily.

Later, Roc recovered, and as he staggered up the hillside, Ute behind him, the sudden crack of rifles cut the freezing air. With bullets whipping up snow around them, the three rams sped away, terrified, each in a different direction.

From a distant vantage point, Tor watched their human enemies walking along the swell of a mountain shoulder. Their presence turned the well-being he had felt earlier into a clutching fear.

Tor stayed near the rim rocks a few days longer, bedding down on a ledge above a canyon and feeding on a little mesa. He had just returned to the ledge when the roar of a rifle split the silence, rattling echoes off the rim rocks near him. In a single bound he was down the face of the cliff and across a talus slope, disappearing behind a pillar of rocks where he stayed well-hidden. It was two days before the fear of man began to fade. Yet when hunger gnawed at his belly he was still afraid to go out on the mesa, and fed along the sheer, rugged cliff walls where clumps of dry grass and plants clung to cracks of thin, shallow soil. The tans, browns, and grays of the rocks and earth and the deep crevices of the canyon walls offered protective camouflage for his body.

It was several days more before he left the hiding place, his eyes constantly watchful for movement of any kind. As he circled a cliff of jutting ledges, he came face to face with a big bobcat. Tor snorted. The bobcat humped its back and snarled, then ran away, vanishing into a brushy cliff beyond. Tor shook his head angrily, then continued circling the cliff. It was not until he crossed a spur-ridge that he saw Roc lying on a ledge that sloped down to a deep, snow-covered ravine. Hurrying to Roc's side, Tor sniffed the older ram's feverishly panting body. Roc tried to raise his head, his breath a soft whisper of pain that beaded his lips with tiny bubbles of blood. Tor could not know that an over anxious hunter had only wounded instead of killing Roc. The older ram had run until his strength failed. Now he lay slowly bleeding to death.

Tor sniffed the spreading trickles of blood crystallizing on the snow, then stepped back and leaped on a small, rocky bluff that jutted out of the timbered hillside. Here he would stand guard. Roc was no longer a foe but a crippled member of his herd in need of protection.

As darkness settled over the mountains, stars began to prick the sky. The moon was a yellow disk of light that beamed palely from behind a filmy veil of clouds. Tor watched for moving shadows against the snowy hillside, but the world seemed lifeless.

The next morning he saw a cougar hiding in a patch of brush and pines at the mouth of a ravine. He stepped quickly behind a jumble of rocks, where he could peek through an open fissure, and watched it move stealthily toward the ledge. The dangerous horns were held low, the heavy body tense, ready to leap to one side and charge. Each hair stood up stiff and turned toward his head, making him look twice his size.

The big, one-hundred-fifty-pound cougar crept closer, its tawny belly scraping the snowy ground, its eyes fastened on its helpless prey. With lips drawn back in a snarl, whiskers twitching, ears erect and thrust forward, head moving slowly, cautiously from side to side in order to catch the slightest movement or sound, the cougar stopped, crouched—and sprang.

Tor leaped to meet it, three hundred pounds of striking force behind horns that smashed into the startled face of the cougar. Spitting and growling with rage and pain the cougar struck back, its knife-like claws extended, raking furrows along the base of one horn. The cougar turned to strike again, but Tor leaped aside. With horns held low to protect his throat, he hit the cougar a glancing blow that knocked it backwards down the slope, kicking and spitting.

The cougar got to its feet and stared at Tor with an expression of murderous fury—and surprise. It had neither seen nor scented this dangerous enemy. The odor from the dying ram had been too strong. With deep, menancing growls it moved up the slope a few steps, then turned slowly and melted into the dense underbrush of the ravine.

Tor walked back and forth for several minutes, grunting and blowing out snorts of anger as he peered after it. He lost sight of the cougar and returned to Roc, but this time there was no sign of recognition in the older ram's staring, sightless eyes. Tor stood beside him for a moment, unable to challenge the finality of death. Then he sniffed the cold air up-wind, anxious to return to the ewe-band, to be once again a member of his own herd, and to be the leader.

As he started along the rocky bluff that jutted out of the timbered hillside, a sixth sense made him stop and look up. Descending on him was the cougar, its body flying straight down like a giant arrow!

Tor turned to run. But it was too late. The cougar landed on his back, one forepaw reaching for his muzzle. Terror whipped Tor's head to one side, and the deadly paw missed. Tor tried to shake off the cougar, but it clung to his back, its teeth sunk in his neck, its claws shredding his flesh. Despite the blinding pain he made a sudden powerful lunge that catapulted them down the hillside, over a high bluff and into a deep ravine, breaking the cougar's hold. Tor fell on top of the cougar, his three-hundred-pound body crushing its belly, snapping its spine. Half-conscious, he lay across the cougar, his sides, back and lacerated neck muscles a well of pain that finally made him aware of the motionless body beneath him. Struggling to his feet, he looked down at the paralyzed cougar, its mouth open, its pink tongue hanging limply over long, ripping fangs. For one tense moment their eyes met. Then Tor leaned forward, powerful horns poised over its jugular vein, ready to kill.

The wildness in his eyes suddenly misted over with indecision. Stepping back slowly, painfully, he staggered through the spreading patterns of red in the churned-up snow, then fell heavily to the ground, the once brilliant eyes glazed with pain, the tip of his tongue thrust between his lips, siphoning agonizing breaths from the depths of his lungs. He forced himself to his feet and step by step toward a hiding place in a covert of heavy brush. But the hill proved too high, his body too weak. He sank to the ground, his head dropping to his breast. The fevered panting of his breath stirred little eddies of powdered snow around his nostrils.

Tor was unconscious for several peaceful minutes, then his eyes opened slowly. As they began to focus on the cold, white world around him, two shadows moved up the hillside. He studied the shadows, and a spark of light returned out of the long, dark corridor of pain. Forcing his torn and bleeding body to its full height, Tor stared down at his human enemies, unafraid. The bullet, its echoes reverberating across the canyon in plaintive circles of sound, shocked his life into silence, leaving the big head at a twisted angle, one great horn buried in the snow-covered earth, the beautiful amber-colored eyes opened wide to the distant hills of a familiar homeland he could no longer see.